3/17/21

MARGARET & FAMILY

THANK you FOR All ~~with~~ YouR
HELP!
STAY SAFE & STAY WELL!

Audrey
Nancy Pierce
Gingery

The Little Floofs' Book of Money

Written By: Audrey B. Daum
Illustrated by: Jamie P. Harper

ISBN 978-1-09834-565-5

ACKNOWLEDGEMENTS

I want to thank a number of people who contributed to this book. My partner in crime and illustrator, Jamie Harper, who made this evolving story come to life with his precious drawings. His patience and sense of humor have been a delight. We share a mutual passion for all creatures and Samoyeds in particular. I fell in love with his amazing work on the Samoyed Fans' Facebook page where we are both members.

Also, I want to thank my very close friends who read multiple drafts and contributed to the story idea and my late parents, without whom I would not have the perseverance and determination to get this done. They both had writing and editorial talent and urged me to develop mine. An additional thanks to Heidi Pickett, Assistant Dean, Master of Finance Program at MIT Sloan School who supported the idea, wrote the Foreword and who sits on the Board of Invest in Girls.

Samoyeds are a very special breed of dog, well known the world over for their beauty, their gentle nature, and happy smile. They have a specific attachment to children of all ages and are well loved by them. I was a long-time admirer of Jamie's work which is displayed on the Samoyed Fans Facebook Page and partnered with him to illustrate this light hearted book.

FOREWORD

Financial literacy is a life skill that can make or break a young person's future. According to the Council for Economic Education, more than 1 in 6 students do not reach the baseline level of proficiency in financial literacy. In the U.S., only a portion of States require personal finance for high school students to graduate. That's too little and far too late – financial lessons need to be introduced early in life so that children can grow into financially responsible adults capable of navigating essential money matters.

With many thanks to Audrey Daum and her clever introduction to the concept of money, parents and teachers now have a delightful story to teach the important lessons of saving. The illustrations are fun and the reader cannot help but fall in love with The Floofs, particularly Saver Susie. The messages on how you acquire and spend money are easy to understand for a child first learning about financial concepts and are relatable to all ages. Equally important, Audrey extends the idea of saving for the future and how savings can be put to good use for education or helping others.

As a parent and an advocate for financial literacy, I highly recommend The Little Floofs' Book of Money as a great tool to help educate all children in the concept of money and provide them the necessary beginnings of financial literacy.

Heidi V. Pickett

Assistant Dean, MIT Sloan Master of Finance Program

Board of Director, Invest in Girls, a program of the Council For Economic Education

THE LITTLE FLOOFS' BOOK OF MONEY

The Floofs are a family like many others

Cute and fluffy two sisters and a brother

Susie saves her coins and bills

While Spender Sam, he spends at will

Sister Susie is the saver you see

Because dog toys and treats don't grow on trees

Coins are pretty they shimmer and shine

Made out of metal they're yours and they're mine

Fancy Phoebe saves nothing at all
While always buying toys and balls

But Saver Susie uses cash with care
And Sam and Phoebe have none to spare

They add up to bills so save them it pays

In time you will need them for those rainy days

Does cash grow on trees or under your bed?

More likely you've earned it with jobs instead

It can come as a gift, it can come from your chores

You can use it for snacks, for books, and more

You can buy food, a ball, or even a doll

If you have no cash, can't buy nothing at all

So save it, spend it, or share it with friends

But don't spend it all, because it's not without end

Spend · Save · Share

It can come as a coin, as a bill, or a card

If nothing is saved, life will be very hard

You can buy some treats or find ways to share
But without it remember that your cupboards
are bare

You can save in a pillow, a toy pig, or a bank
If it comes as a gift, don't forget who to thank

Put it away, make it safe, make it sound

You don't want to leave too much cash all around

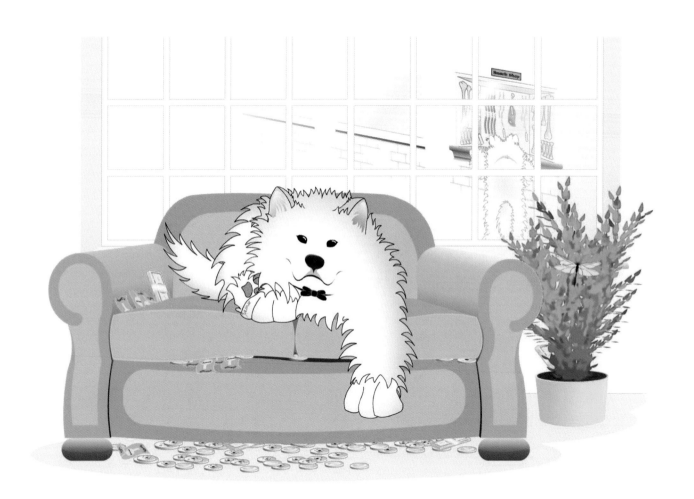

Change can be pennies, nickels, and dimes

Two dimes and a nickel make a quarter you'll find

Dollars are green with letters of white

A pile of bills can be quite a sight

Save a hundred pennies to make a quick buck

For without a dollar you will have little luck

9

To buy dog food, a leash, or even a chop
without a dollar your fortune will drop

Snack Shop

To have an allowance you work hard and behave

And then with time those dollars you'll save

Can help you buy the things you need

There are so many places a dollar can lead

To buy dog toys, presents, or even a pup

In time if you save those dollars add up

Small amounts can be kept in a wallet or purse

Keep it quite safe for losing it's worse

Because when it comes to the money you lose

The money is gone and you can't choose

Best kept in a bank where it's in a safe place

Don't want to lose money without a trace

You can get it by check you can get it by card

Taking some out will not be very hard

Saving is something you do every day

For your very own future your savings will pay

If you leave it to stay and to grow each day

Your money will be there for that rainy day

It can help you with needs it can help you with wants

It can help you with school and can help you with jaunts

If all your money is more than you need

Invest your money and see where it leads

If someday you're lucky and reach all your goals
You'll be able to share with some needy souls

You can help with the sick and can help with the poor

Money can open some life changing doors

Susie started saving as a kid you see

So she has cash in a bank to help all three

The cash you save can help to feed

Your friends and family and all you need

When Sam was sick and had vet bills to pay
Saver Susie was there to save the day

And when Phoebe needed a new dog house for play
Saver Susie was able to help her pay

And then there were pups that Susie knew

who needed to get some dog bones to chew

They lived in a Shelter that was not far away

Because they had nowhere else to stay

Susie has always had as a goal

To help the pups with no food in their bowl

Spender Sam too has a goal to reach

To go to pup school where they will teach

New tricks and things like sit and stay

But for the school he has to pay

So little by little he puts cash away

And learns to save for that rainy day

Someday soon Sam will go to that school

And not have to borrow from Saver Sue

Fancy Phoebe goes each day, visits the shelter and plays

Her friends all live together and are happy to see her stay

The Shelter helps the pups and cats who need a home you see
They give them food and lots of love and a lovely place to be

One day in spring the Floofs find out their friends are out of luck
The shelter doesn't have the cash to stay, not even a single buck

Saver Susie wants to help but can't do it on her own
Both Sam and Phoebe too decide their friends must keep their home

So Phoebe is the Floof that had the least cash saved to pay
But every day she bought fewer balls and put the cash away

24

Soon all three Floofs had saved and saved and had a pile of cash
   To give the Shelter what they need the Floofs have saved a stash

The cash was used to have a day when rescue floofs could come and play

Sam always wanted a brother you see

So he saved up for the adoption fee

They called him Scratch cause he had an itch

No matter what he had to twitch

So after a very careful vetting

Scratch came home for lots of petting

So here you see the story ends that saving is the way

You never know when cash you have will somehow save the day

LEARNING ACTIVITIES

1. Saver Susie is out of dog food . A bag will cost $1.00.

How many pennies does it take for a bag of dog food?

How many dimes does it take for a bag of dog food?

2. Fancy Phoebe wants to get new balls. They cost $3.00.

How many quarters will it take to buy the balls?

(Hint: One dollar=Four quarters)

3. Spender Sam wants to get a puppy ice cream. It costs $5.00.

How many single dollars does he need to save to get his puppy ice cream.

4. Saver Susie wants to bring a bag of treats to the Floof Shelter. It costs $1.00.

How many nickels does she have to save to buy the treats.

(Hint: 5 cents = 1 nickel

Color Us In